The Adventures of Frankie

The Hound Dog

Sadie's First Birthday

Written and Illustrated by

Patricia Anne Rose

The Adventures of Frankie the Hound Dog
Sadie's First Birthday
Copyright © 2023
by written and illustrated by Patricia Anne Rose

ISBN: 978-1-954253-98-8

First Edition / Full Color

Printed in the United States of America

Dedication

To Dad, Richard F. Rose, who loved my owl painting – that was how it all began. I promised you I would write a story. Just sorry it took so long.

And to . . .

Mom, Katherine M. Saeman, who spent many hours with me in Cape Cod to create this story.

I hope you can both see this book through the midst of the Milky Way.

And, goes without saying, my three grandgirls:

Eila

Bernice

Piper

IT WAS THE EVENING OF JUNE 13TH.
THE SUN WAS GOING DOWN AND ALL
THE NIGHTTIME CRITTERS OF THE
FOREST WERE JUST WAKING UP,
BUT ...

FRANKIE THE HOUND DOG WAS GETTING
READY FOR BED.

HE LIVED WITH A MAN NAMED BUTCH

WHO LIVED IN THE WOODS.

THE FIRE FLIES WERE MERRILY
SINGING WHILE LIGHTING UP
THE DARK SKY UNDER THE
MILKY WAY.

YOU CAN HEAR THE FROGS
CROAKING DOWN AT THE
POND.

MRS. BATTY WAS MAKING HER
BABIES BREAKFAST FOR
TONIGHT,

THE TWINS WERE GOING TO
HAVE THEIR FIRST FLYING
LESSON IN CLASS.

MAMA DOG, MS. ROSE, WAS
GETTING HER PUPS
BREAKFAST AS THEY WERE
GETTING READY FOR SCHOOL.
SADIE WAS THE YOUNGEST
PUPPY AND TODAY WAS HER
1ST BIRTHDAY.

THE PUPS YELPED, "BYE MA,"
AS THEY LEFT FOR THE
SCHOOL BUS.

ON THEIR WAY TO SCHOOL,
THEY SAW MR. WHOO.

HE ALWAYS WATCHED OUT
FOR THE CHILDREN, MAKING
SURE THEY GOT TO SCHOOL
SAFELY.

MISS OLIVE,

THE SCHOOL TEACHER,

DID NOT LIKE ANY ONE TO BE

LATE FOR HER CLASS.

ABCDEFG
HIJKLMNOPQ
RSTUVWXYZ
2 +2 4
3 +3 6
4 +4 8
5 +5 10
6 +6 12
7 +7 14
8 +8 16
9 +9 18
10 +10 20
Miss Olive
ROSE

IN THE MEANTIME,
THE OYSTERS IN THE POND
WERE HAPPILY MAKING A
PEARL NECKLACE
FOR A VERY SPECIAL
OCCASION.

ROSE

BLUE-EYED JACK WATCHED

WHILE MRS. SILK WORM

HELPED BY TYING THE PEARLS

TOGETHER.

EVERYONE WAS HELPING

PREPARE

FOR SADIE'S

BIRTHDAY PARTY.

WHEN SADIE WALKED INTO
SCHOOL,
HER FRIENDS STOPPED
TALKING.

SHE BECAME SAD BECAUSE
SHE THOUGHT THEY WERE
TALKING ABOUT HER.

SADIE WAS SAD ALL THROUGH
CLASS.
AFTER SCHOOL, INSTEAD OF
GOING HOME, SHE WALKED
DEEP INTO THE FOREST.

WHEN SADIE DIDN'T COME
HOME WITH HER BROTHERS
AND SISTER, MAMA DOG, MS.
ROSE, WAS WORRIED.

...ALLED:

MRS. WOLF

MISS OLIVE

AND

MR. WHOO

BUT NONE OF THEM HAD SEEN

LITTLE SADIE.

...NKIE THE HOUND

...COULD FIND ANYONE WITH

HIS

POWERFUL SMELLING NOSE.

FRANKIE WAS HAPPY

TO HELP. SO ...

HE SET OUT INTO THE WOODS WITH HIS NOSE

TO THE GROUND, LOOKING AND SNIFFING FOR

LITTLE SADIE.

HE PICKED UP HER SCENT AND FOLLOWED IT

THROUGH THE WOODS.

THE BABY DEER.

ASKED KATIE,

YOU SEEN LITTLE SADIE?"

"NO FRANKIE, I HAVE NOT."

THEN FRANKIE SAW MR. & MRS. TOM NEAR THE
MEADOW. HE ASKED,

"HAVE YOU SEEN LITTLE SADIE?"

"NO FRANKIE, WE HAVE NOT."

NOT SEEN

DIE EITHER.

FRANKIE CONTINUED HIS
JOURNEY AND FOUND SADIE
CRYING NEAR A TREE LOG.

FRANKIE ASKED HER,
"WHY ARE YOU CRYING?"

SADIE SAID,
"MY FRIENDS AT SCHOOL WERE
TALKING ABOUT ME."

"THERE NOW SADIE. YOUR
FRIENDS & FAMILY ARE ALL
WORRIED ABOUT YOU. LET'S
GO BACK AND LET THEM KNOW
YOU ARE SAFE."

SADIE AGREED.

IN THE MEANTIME . . .

EVERYONE WAS AT THE PARTY PREPARING THE FOOD AND DECORATIONS WHEN THEY SAW FRANKIE LEADING SADIE DOWN THE PATH.

"LOOK! SADIE IS HOME SAFE!"

"HIP HIP HURRAY!"

SADIE WAS SO SURPRISED TO SEE EVERYONE. SHE THOUGHT . . . *SO THAT'S WHY MY FRIENDS STOPPED TALKING WHEN THEY SAW ME AT SCHOOL TODAY. THEY WERE PLANNING MY BIRTHDAY PARTY!*

AT THE PARTY

THEY ALL SANG AND DANCED AND HAD SO MUCH FUN.

SADIE LOVED HER PEARL NECKLACE AND ALL OF HER

PRESENTS BUT,

WHEN SHE BLEW OUT THE CANDLE ...

INSTEAD OF MAKING A WISH,

SADIE THOUGHT ...

I AM SO THANKFUL TO BE WITH

MY FAMILY AND FRIENDS

AND

FRANKIE WILL ALWAYS BE

MY HERO!

JUST THEN, A SHOOTING STAR

STREAKED ACROSS THE NIGHT

SKY

UNDER THE MILKY WAY

THE END

ABOUT THE AUTHOR

Patricia Anne Rose was born in New York but has resided in Vermont for the past 30 years. Patricia is a semi-retired Registered Nurse who has enjoyed her career. She has two grown children, Charles and Brookley, and three grand girls whom she enjoys immensely.

As a child, her favorite past time was adventure walks in the woods with her dad and brother, always looking for owls and little critters. Beauty and the respect for nature was instilled during those special walks.

Later in life, Patricia painted a picture of an owl. After much encouragement from her family, especially her dad, she was inspired to create a children's story. This is where Frankie the Hound Dog's idea was born. Frankie and Sadie are two real dogs, and this is where the story began.

Please visit the Author at:

www.frankiethehounddog.com

to connect with the author and watch for
Frankie's Next Adventure.

About the

MILKY WAY:

THE MILKY WAY IS A GALAXY WHICH INCLUDES OUR SOLAR SYSTEM.

IT IS A HAZY BAND OF LIGHT SEEN IN THE NIGHT SKY FORMED FROM STARS.

LOOK FOR THE MILKY WAY IN SOME OF THE PICTURES IN THIS VERY BOOK!

DRAW YOUR FAVORITE BIRTHDAY HAT

DRAW YOUR FAVORITE BIRTHDAY CAKE

DRAW YOUR FAVORITE
CRITTER FROM THIS BOOK

DRAW YOURSELF ON A
WALK WITH FRANKIE AND SADIE

MISS OLIVE IS MY FAVORITE TEACHER

DRAW YOUR FAVORITE TEACHER

DRAW THE MILKY WAY

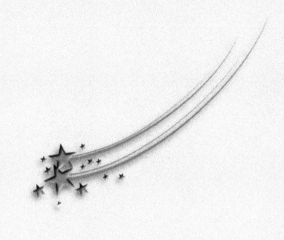

CPSIA information can be obtained
at www.ICGtesting.com
Printed in the USA
JSHW071202230523
42083JS00001B/1

9 781954 253988